First published in Japan in 1983 by Child Honsha Co., Ltd. under the title *Nezumi no Kaisuiyoku*.
First published in the United States, Great Britain, Canada, Australia, and New Zealand in 2012
by North-South Books Inc., New York 10017, an imprint of NordSüd Verlag AG, CH-8005 Zürich, Switzerland.
Translated by Missy Debs and Masako Irie.
Distributed in the United States by North-South Books Inc., New York 10017.
Library of Congress Cataloging-in-Publication Data is available.
Printed in Germany by Grafisches Centrum Cuno GmbH & Co. KG, 39240 Calbe, November 2011.
ISBN: 978-0-7358-4073-7 (trade edition)
1 3 5 7 9 • 10 8 6 4 2

www.northsouth.com

FSC
www.fsc.org
MIX
Paper from
responsible sources
FSC® C043106

Seven Little Mice
Go to the Beach

by Haruo Yamashita

illustrated by

Kazuo Iwamura

NorthSouth
New York / London

This is the story of seven little mice. They are septuplets, which is like twins only there are seven.

The seven little mice went to school all year long. But there was no school tomorrow. It was the first day of summer vacation!

"Tomorrow we'll all go to the beach together," said Father.

The seven little mice jumped for joy. "I can swim the crawl." "I can do the breaststroke." "I'm going surfing." "I'll water ski." "I'll go fishing." "I'll do the dog paddle." "And I'll do the mouse paddle!"

Father said, "You children are good little swimmers, but we need to be safe in the water."

So Father made seven life preservers. Then he tied a rope to each one.

The next day was bright and clear. The mice packed a lunch, hopped on the train, and were off to the beach.

"Uh-oh! This beach is too crowded. It'd be easy for the seven little mice to get lost here," Father said. "I wonder if we can find someplace more quiet."

The seven little mice found a little inlet away from the crowd.

"Hmmm! That rock would be good for a lookout," said Father. "This is perfect!"

The seven little mice changed into their swimsuits and jumped into the water. "What fun to be at the beach!"

Swimming mice, fishing mice, surfing mice . . . everybody felt safe with
Father and Mother watching them.

"How about taking a rest and having some lunch?" Mother called out.

Mmmm! Mother's rice balls were delicious.

After lunch it was nap time. The breeze from the sea felt just right.

But the tide had rolled in.

"Oh, no!" cried the seven little mice. "Father is stranded!"

Everyone called to Father, "Come back! Come back!"
But Father replied with a puzzled look, "Uh-oh! The water is too deep now. I actually can't swim as well as you and Mother."

"Wait, Father, we'll rescue you with a life preserver," the seven little mice shouted.

But Mother shook her head. "No, no. That life preserver will be too small for Father. He'll sink with it."

"I have a better idea. Let's tie all of the life preservers together.
Then Father can float on them."

"Father, here you go. Now you can float back to shore."

"Oh, thank you!" said Father. "Now it's time for me to take swimming lessons!"

"Heave-ho! Heave-ho! Hooray!"

On the way home, Mother said, "Let's all go to the beach again!"